This journal Belongs To :

From :

Made in the USA
Monee, IL
11 August 2021

75438303R00056